This book belongs to...

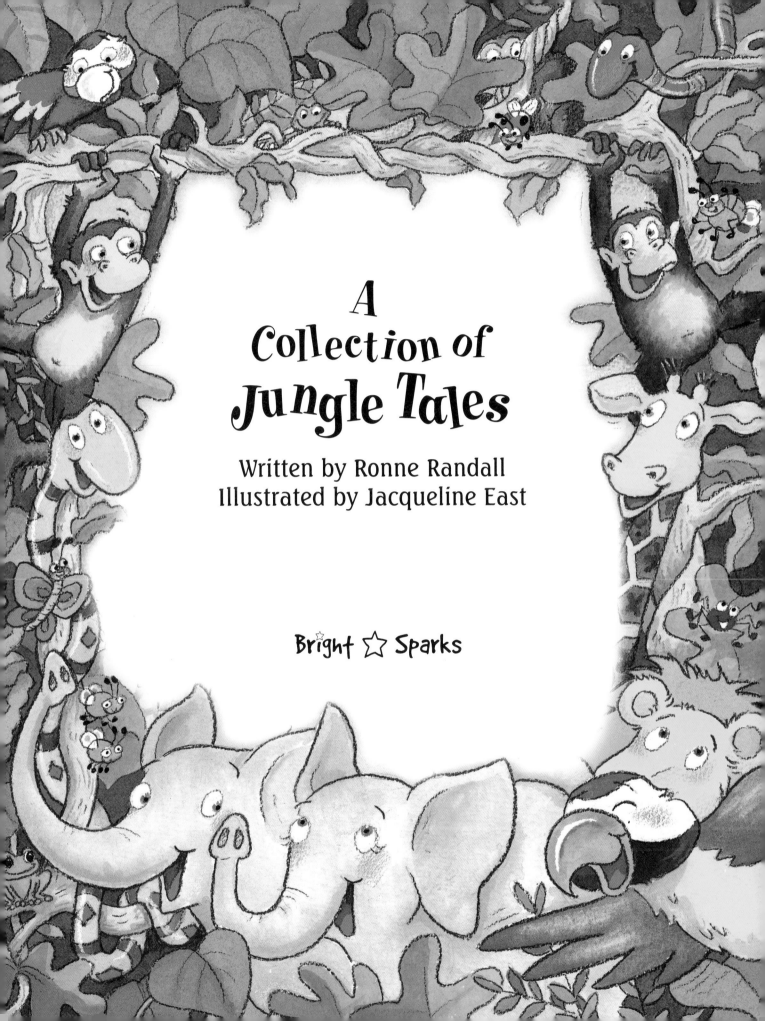

# A Collection of Jungle Tales

Written by Ronne Randall
Illustrated by Jacqueline East

**Bright ☆ Sparks**

This is a Bright Sparks Book
First published in 2001
BRIGHT SPARKS, Queen Street House, 4 Queen Street, Bath
BA1 1HE, UK

Copyright © PARRAGON 2001

Created and produced by THE COMPLETE WORKS

Printed in China

ISBN 1-84250-397-9

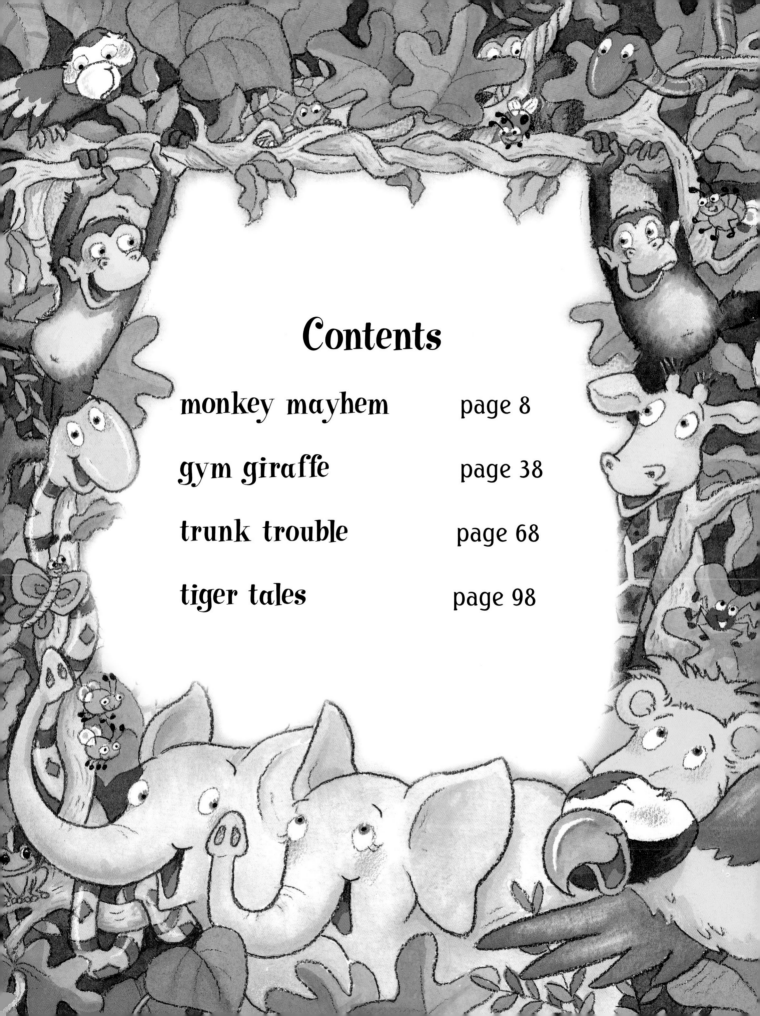

# Contents

# monkey mayhem

Mickey and Maxine Monkey had finished their breakfast of Mango Munch. Now they were rushing off to play.

"Be careful!" called their mom. "And DON'T make too much noise!"

"We won't!" the two mischevious monkeys promised, leaping across to the next tree.

"WHEEEE," screeched Mickey.

"WA-HOOOO!" hollered Maxine.

The noise echoed through the whole jungle—
Mickey and Maxine just didn't know how to be quiet!

KA-THUNK! Mickey landed on a branch.

KA-CLUNK!

Maxine landed beside him.

the monkeys hollered as the branch snapped in two.

they shrieked, as they went tumbling down, down, down.

# KER-THUMMPPP!
## SPROI-OI-OING!

The jungle shook as the two monkeys crashed to the ground, then sprang to their feet.

"YIPPPEEEEEE!" the monkeys cheered, brushing themselves off.

"That was so much FUN!" exclaimed Maxine. "Let's go get Chico Chimp and see if he wants to do it, too!"

Chattering as they went, the two monkeys scrambled back up to the tree tops.

"HEY, CHICO! COME AND PLAY WITH US!" they bellowed as they swung through the branches toward the chimps' house.

All through the jungle, animals shook their heads and covered their ears. Couldn't anyone keep those naughty, noisy monkeys quiet?

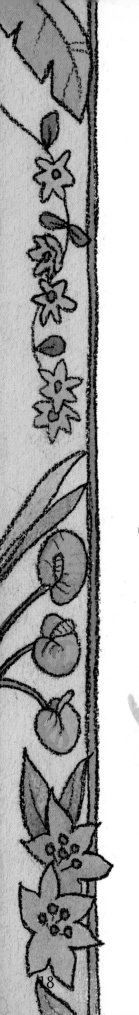

Chico Chimp was soon ready to play with his friends. The three of them had a great time swinging, tumbling, and bouncing together. Then they spotted a coconut palm.

"Hey!" shouted Chico. "Let's get some coconuts!"

"Great!" said Maxine. "Last one up the tree is a rotten banana!"

But before they got to the coconut palm, they stopped short. Grandpa Gorilla was standing in their path, glaring at them angrily.

"Get going, you mischief-makers," he said. "You've given everyone enough headaches for one day. My grandson Gulliver is fast asleep down by the river, and if you wake him up, I will be very, very upset!"

"Sorry," whispered Maxine, looking down at the ground. Everyone in the jungle knew it was a big mistake to upset Grandpa Gorilla!

"We'll be quiet," the three friends promised.

Mickey, Maxine, and Chico slowly wandered away. As they got nearer the coconut palm, Mickey said, "Let's just climb the tree. We can do that quietly."

"Okay," the others agreed halfheartedly.

"I suppose it's better than doing nothing," said Maxine.

From their perch up among the coconuts, the three friends could see what was happening all over the jungle.

They saw Jerome Giraffe showing his son Jeremy how to choose the juiciest, most tender leaves on a tree...

...and they saw Portia Parrot giving her daughter Penelope her first flying lesson.

And right below them, they saw little Gulliver Gorilla sleeping contentedly in the tall grass beside the river.

And – uh-oh! They saw something else, too. Claudia Crocodile was in the river. She was grinning and snapping her big, sharp teeth – and heading straight for Gulliver!

The three friends didn't think twice. Maxine shouted,

# "GET UP, GULLIVER! GET UP RIGHT NOOOOWW!"

At the same time, Mickey and Chico began throwing coconuts at Claudia.

SMAACCCKK!

THWAACKK!

went the coconuts.

they went, right on Claudia's hard crocodile head.

"OWW-WOOWW"

moaned Claudia.

"OWW-WOW OWW-WOW!"

"What's going on here?" Grandpa Gorilla shouted up into the coconut tree. "I thought I told you three to keep quiet!"

All the noise woke Gulliver. The little gorilla sat up, looked around, and ran to his grandpa, who was hurrying toward the river.

Then he saw Claudia swimming away, and he realized what had happened. He grabbed Gulliver and gave him a great big gorilla hug. "I'm so glad you're safe!" he said.

Maxine, Mickey, and Chico came down from the tree.

"We're sorry we made so much noise," Chico said.

By this time all the other gorillas had gathered round, and so had most of the other jungle animals.

"What's all the commotion about?"
asked Jerome Giraffe.

"Yes, what's going on?" squawked
Portia Parrot.

"These three youngsters are heroes," said Grandpa. "They saved my grandson from being eaten by Claudia Crocodile!"

"Hurrah!" cheered all the other animals. Mrs. Monkey and Mrs. Chimp beamed with pride.

"I think you deserve a reward," said Grandpa Gorilla. "And I think your reward should be…"

All the other animals held their breath in anticipation.

"...permission to be just as noisy as you like, whenever you like!" Grandpa announced.

"YIPP

# PEEEEE!"

cheered Mickey, Maxine, and Chico, in their loudest, screechiest voices. Their grins were almost as wide as the river.

## "OH, NOOOOOO!"

all the other animals groaned together – but they were all smiling, too.

gym
giraffe

Jeremy Giraffe loved going out with his dad to gather juicy green leaves for dinner.

"This is where you find the most delicious leaves, Jeremy," said Dad, reaching wa-a-a-y UP to a very high branch.
"Remember – the tallest trees have the tastiest leaves, and the tiny top leaves are the tenderest!"

41

One morning, Jeremy decided it was time he went out to gather leaves on his own.

"The tallest trees have the tastiest leaves," he whispered to himself as he trotted along, "and the tiny top leaves are the tenderest."

Jeremy stopped at the tallest tree he could find, and looked up. Sure enough, right at the top, there were some tiny, tender leaves just waiting to be plucked.

# Stre-e-e-e-etching

his neck just as he had seen his dad do, Jeremy reached as high as he could – it wasn't very high!

"Oh, dear," he thought. "How will I ever reach the tastiest, tenderest, tiny top leaves if my neck won't stretch?"

So Jeremy went back home with his neck hanging down in despair.

"Why, Jeremy, whatever is the matter?" asked his mom. When Jeremy told her, she gave his neck a nuzzle.

"You're still growing," she assured him. "Just eat your greens and get lots of sleep, and your neck will soon be long enough to reach the tastiest, tiniest, tenderest leaves on the tallest tree tops in the jungle!"

Jeremy couldn't wait for his neck to grow. That afternoon, he rushed out to try again.

High above him, Portia Parrot saw Jeremy struggling to reach the tiny leaves at the top of the tree. "He needs some help," she thought, so she swooped down and plucked a few of the tenderest leaves for him.

When Portia gave Jeremy the leaves, his spots went pale with shame and embarrassment.

"I should be able to get those myself," he wailed. "Why won't my neck stretch?"

"Oh, Jeremy," said Portia, "your neck is just fine! It's still growing, that's all. Just keep eating your greens and getting lots of sleep, and it will grow!"

"But I can't wait," Jeremy insisted. "Isn't there anything I can do to make my neck long and stretchy now?"

"Perhaps there is," said Portia. "I think I know just the place to do it. Follow me, Jeremy!"

Portia led Jeremy through the jungle to a clearing.
Jeremy's eyes widened with wonder at what he saw.
There was so much going on!

Seymour Snake was wrapping himself round and round a fallen tree trunk. "Hello, Jeremy," he hissed.

"Jusssssst doing

my sssssslithering exercisessssss!"

Nearby, Eric and Ellen Elephant were hoisting heavy logs. "One, two, three, LIFT!" they chanted together.

"Hi, Jeremy!" called Eric. "We're just doing our trunk-strengthening workout."

Near the riverbank, Grandpa Gorilla was holding out thick branches for Claudia Crocodile to break in half.

"Just limbering up my jaw muscles," Claudia snapped.

Leonard Lion was taking his own cubs, Louis and Lisa, through their pouncing paces. "Welcome to the Jungle Gym, Jeremy!" he called.

A few minutes later, Grandpa Gorilla and Leonard Lion came to greet Jeremy. "What can we do for you?" they asked.

"My neck is too short," said Jeremy. "Can you help me stretch it? I want to be able to reach the tasty, tiny, tender leaves at the tops of the trees, just like my dad does."

"You're still growing," said Leonard Lion. "Just eat up all your greens, get lots of sleep, and your neck will grow."

Jeremy's face fell. But he brightened up when Grandpa Gorilla said, "In the meantime, we can give you a special program of neck-stretching exercises to help things along. Come with us!"

Grandpa got Jeremy started right away.

"S-t-r-e-t-c-h to the left!
S-t-r-e-t-c-h to the right!"

Grandpa Gorilla shouted.

"Left!

Left!

Right!

Right!"

"Chin lifts next," said Leonard Lion. Jeremy s-t-r-e-e-e-t-c-h-e-d as far as he could to get his chin onto the branch.

"Come on, you can do it!" Portia said, cheering him on.

"I think Seymour can help with the next one," said Grandpa Gorilla. "Jeremy, you get down on the ground, and Seymour – start slithering!"

# "Aaaakkk!"

gasped Jeremy, as
Seymour wrapped himself
round his neck.

"Er… not quite so tight, Seymour," said Grandpa

"Aaaaahh!" sighed Jeremy. "That's better!"
Seymour slithered along, pu-u-u-l-l-ing
Jeremy's neck muscles as he went.

All the exercise made Jeremy really hungry. At supper that evening, he had three B<sub>I</sub>G helpings of greens.

He was tired, too, so he went to bed early and slept soundly all night.

Jeremy couldn't wait to get back to the Jungle Gym and do some more neck-stretching exercises. He went back the next day, the day after that, and the day after that.

"You're making excellent progress, Jeremy," Leonard Lion told him.

Every evening after his workout, Jeremy ate a good supper.

"Exercising makes me soooo hungry…" he told his mum and dad…

"and soOOO tired," he yawned, as he settled down to sleep.

A few days later, Jeremy and his dad went out leaf-gathering together. Suddenly, Jeremy spotted a brand-new bunch of succulent, sweet-looking leaves right at the top of a tall tree.

"I'm going to get those, Dad," he said.

"But Jeremy," said Dad, "they're so high up!"

Jeremy didn't hear him. He was too busy stretching... and

and...

stre-e-e-e-e-tching...

s
t
r
e
e
t
c
h
i
n
g...

...until he stretched right up to the very top branch!

"I've done it, Dad!" he cried happily. "The exercises worked!"

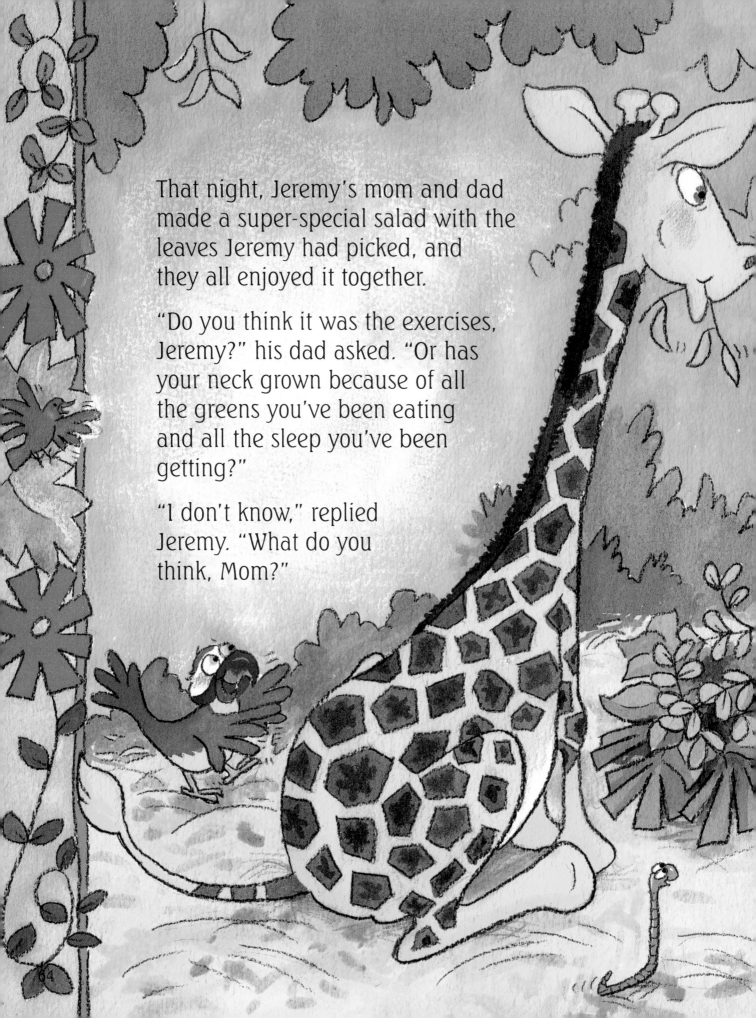

That night, Jeremy's mom and dad made a super-special salad with the leaves Jeremy had picked, and they all enjoyed it together.

"Do you think it was the exercises, Jeremy?" his dad asked. "Or has your neck grown because of all the greens you've been eating and all the sleep you've been getting?"

"I don't know," replied Jeremy. "What do you think, Mom?"

"I think it doesn't matter at all," replied Mom. "What matters is that you have a fine, strong, **lo-o-o-o-ng** neck that any giraffe would be proud of!"

"And I am!" said Jeremy, taking another mouthful of tasty, tender leaves. He chewed the leaves extra thoroughly – because he knew they had a very long way to go!

# trunk trouble

Emma, Ellen, and Eric Elephant had spent nearly all day at the river, splashing and sploshing in the cool, clear water and giving each other excellent elephant showers.

But now it was nearly dinner time, and their rumbling
tummies told them it was time to head for home.

71

First the little elephants had to dry themselves off.
They made their way out to the clearing, and carefully
dusted themselves with fine earth and sand.

WHOOSH!      WHOOSH!
PUFFLE!

went Ellen with her trunk.

PUFFLE!    PUFFLE!   WHOOSH!

went Emma with her trunk.
Both sisters had long, graceful trunks,
and they were very proud of them.

WHOOSH! PUFFLE!
WHOOSH...
PUFF!

went Eric, when his
sisters' backs were turned.

COUGH!          COUGH!

AH-CHOO!

went Emma and Ellen.
"Hey! Cut it out!" they
shouted.

Eric just giggled. He loved annoying his sisters.

71

"I'll race you home!" Eric called, when they were all dry. "Last one back is an elephant egg!" And he loped back into the jungle.

Ellen and Emma ran after him. "We'll get there first! We'll beat you!" they cried, going as quickly as they could.

Ellen and Emma were running so fast and trying so hard to catch up with their brother that they forgot to look where they were going.

All at once, Emma's feet got caught in a leafy, trailing vine, and she stumbled and lost her balance.

**"Oh-oh-OOOOHHHH!"** she cried as she slipped and staggered and started to fall.

"Grab my trunk!" Ellen cried, reaching out to her sister.

But Emma grabbed her sister's trunk so hard that she pulled Ellen down with her. As the two elephants struggled to straighten up, their trunks got twisted together in a great big tangle.

"Help!" they cried. "Eric! Help!"

When their brother turned and saw what had happened, he came bounding back.

"Don't worry!" he called. "I'll save you!"

Eric reached out with his trunk to try to help his sisters up. But the vine leaves were very slippery, and as he grabbed his sisters' trunks, he slipped and lost his balance, too. Now Eric's trunk was all tangled up with Emma's and Ellen's!

The three elephants sat there in a sad, tangled heap. They couldn't straighten out their trunks, they couldn't pull themselves apart – they could hardly even move.

"What are we going to do?" wailed Emma.

"Don't worry, someone will come and help us," Ellen said, trying to reassure her.

"This is all your fault!" Eric grumbled. "If it wasn't for you two, I'd be home by now, eating my dinner!"

A moment later, Seymour Snake came slithering by.

"Greetingsssss," he hissed, looking curiously at the heap of elephants.

"Isss thisss an interesting new game?"

"It's not a game at all!" sobbed Emma. "We're all tangled together and we can't get up. Can you help us, Seymour?"

"Well I'll certainly do my bessst,"

said Seymour.

"Let's see
if I can untwissst you."

He wriggled in
among the tangle of
trunks to see what
he could do.

But everything was so muddled and jumbled together that Seymour couldn't even find his way out!

"Graciousss me!"

he exclaimed.

"I ssseem to be sssstuck!"

"Well, that's just great!" said Eric. "As if we didn't have enough problems – now we have a snake to worry about, too!"

"I ssssuggest you sssstart thinking about a ssssolution to all thissss," Seymour hissed. "I'm not too tangled up to give you a nasssty nip!"

Just then Mickey and Maxine Monkey came swinging through the branches.

"HEY, YOU GUYS!"

they shouted. They weren't very far away – Mickey and Maxine always shouted.

"WHAT'S GOING ON?"

**"We're stuck!"** cried Ellen. "Please help us get untangled so we can go home!"

"Well, we can try pulling you apart," said Maxine, scurrying down to inspect the pile of elephants and snake. "Mickey, you take a tail, and I'll take some ears."

Mickey grabbed hold of Eric's tail, and Maxine gripped Ellen's ears. Then they both pulled and pulled and

# p-u-l-l-e-d.

"OUCH!"

cried Eric.

"OUCH-OUCH-OOUUCCHH!"

bellowed Ellen.

"I'm being ssssqueezzzzed breathlessssss!"

hissed Seymour in alarm.

Mickey and Maxine gave up. Pulling obviously wasn't going to work.

Suddenly there was a flapping up above as Portia Parrot and her daughter Penelope landed in a tree. They had something in their beaks, and as everyone looked up, they let it go. A large cloud of dry, dusty, sandy earth drifted down.

"Cough-cough-ca-choooo!"

spluttered Mickey and Maxine.

"Cough-cough-ca-choooo!"

thundered the elephants.

For a moment, they didn't know what had happened.
Then they realized—they had sneezed themselves apart!

"Thank you," cried the elephants.
"Thank you sssssoooo much!" exclaimed Seymour.

"It was Penelope's idea," said Portia.

"Everyone's invited to our house for dinner!" said Eric.

"Hooray!" cried the others.

With their trunks held high, the elephants led the way back to their house – walking calmly and slowly, and very, **very** carefully!

The End!

tiger
tales

Louis and Lisa Lion were just learning to pounce, and their dad had told them to practice as much as they could. So they were prowling through the jungle, looking for prey to pounce upon.

"There's something orange and blue and fluttery," whispered Lisa. "Here I go…"

# POUNCE!

As Lisa pounced on the butterfly, Louis spotted something green and jumpy. He crept up and got ready to...

**POUNCE!**

Just then, Lisa caught a glimpse of black and yellow fuzz. "Perfect for pouncing," she thought. "Ready, steady…"

103

POUNCE!

"OUCH!"

cried Lisa, rubbing
her nose with her paw.

"Maybe a bumblebee isn't such a good pouncing target! In fact, I think I've had enough pouncing practice for one day."

"Me too," said Louis. "Let's find something else to do."

But as the two little cubs bounded through the jungle, Louis suddenly saw a flash of orange and black in some bushes.

"A striped snake!" he whispered. "It's too good to pass up!" So he crouched down and waited and waited for just the right moment, and then he…

# POUNCED!

# "OWWWOOWW!"

came a voice from the bush. "What's got my tail?"

The 'snake' turned out to be attached to a striped little cub, just the same size as Louis and Lisa!

"Who are you?" they asked.

"I'm Timmy Tiger," said the little cub. "My mom and dad and I have just moved here from The Other Side of the Jungle. Who are you?"

"We're Louis and Lisa Lion," said Lisa. "Would you like to see what this side of the jungle looks like?"

Timmy said he would love to.

"That's our river," said Louis proudly. "It's really muddy, and fun to paddle in."

"It's very nice," said Timmy, "but it's kind of small. On The Other Side of the Jungle, there's a river that's as wide as fifty tall palm trees laid end to end!"

"Gosh!" said Louis and Lisa.

"And I can swim across that river – and back – without stopping once!" added Timmy.

"We can't even swim," said Lisa. "Will you show us how?"

"Err… maybe another time," said Timmy. "I'm just getting over the sniffles, and Mom said I shouldn't swim for a while."

A little farther along, Louis and Lisa saw Howard Hippo wallowing merrily in the mud.

"Hi, Howard!" they called. "This is our new friend, Timmy Tiger!"

Howard opened his mouth in a happy hippo grin. "Nice to meet you!" he bellowed.

"Nice to meet you, too," said Timmy, keeping his distance.

"You know," said Timmy, as the three cubs scampered on, "on The Other Side of the Jungle there's a hippo whose mouth is so big that Mom and Dad and I can all sit inside it!"

"Really?" gasped Louis and Lisa.

"Oh, yes," Timmy assured them. "It's cool and shady in there on hot, sunny days!"

Before Louis and Lisa had a chance to think about that, something dropped down from a branch, right in front of them. Timmy jumped back, but Louis and Lisa smiled and said, "Hi, Seymour! Meet our new friend, Timmy Tiger."

"Greetingsssss," hissed

Seymour Snake. "Ssso niccce to make your aquaintancccce!"

"Nice to meet you, too," said Timmy,
a little uncertainly.
"Well, sssso long," said Seymour,

as he slithered off.
"Sssssee you sssssoon I suppose!"

As Seymour disappeared down the path, Timmy said, "On The Other Side of the Jungle, there are snakes as thick as tree trunks. In fact, when I was a baby, one of those snakes swallowed me whole!"

"Oh, no!" cried Louis and Lisa.

"Yes," Timmy went on, "but my dad saved me by hitting the snake on the head so that he would spit me out!"

"Really?" said Louis and Lisa, their eyes growing wider and wider.

"Yes," said Timmy. "My dad's really, really strong, and really, really big. He's twice as big as an elephant, and he can carry six gorillas on his back! And my mom can do amazing things. She can stand on her front paws and juggle coconuts with her hind legs, and… and…"

"...and what?" asked a smiling, normal-sized tiger, on the path in front of them. Standing next to him – on all four legs – was another smiling tiger.

"...and, here they are," said Timmy, a little sheepishly. "Mom and Dad, these are my new friends, Louis and Lisa Lion."

"We're delighted to meet you," said Mr. and Mrs. Tiger.

"And as you can see," Mrs. Tiger added, "we are very ordinary and normal tigers."

"But what about all those amazing things Timmy told us?" asked Louis. "What about The Other Side of the Jungle?"

"The Other Side of the Jungle is just like this side," said Mr. Tiger.

"You mean the river isn't as wide as fifty tall palm trees laid end to end?" asked Lisa.

"And there isn't a hippo whose mouth is big enough to sit in, or a snake who swallowed Timmy when he was a baby?"

"No, indeed!" laughed Mrs. Tiger.

Timmy looked embarrassed. "Well, they were good stories," he said.

"Yes," said Mrs. Tiger, "but they were just stories." She turned to Louis and Lisa. "Timmy didn't have any friends to play with on The Other Side of the Jungle, so he spent all his time making up fantastic stories and imagining amazing adventures."

"But now that he's got friends like you two to play with," said Mr. Tiger, "perhaps he'll have some real adventures, just as exciting as the ones in his stories!"

"And there are still more friends to meet, Timmy," Lisa said. "Wait till we introduce you to Mickey and Maxine Monkey, and Chico Chimp!"

123

"You know, there are monkeys and chimps on The Other Side of the Jungle, too," said Timmy.

"Really?" said Louis and Lisa, glancing at one another.

"Yes," said Timmy, "but actually, I didn't know them. I can't wait to meet Mickey and Maxine and Chico!"

"Well, what are we waiting for?" said Louis, and the three bounded off together, ready for fun and excitement on *This Side* of the Jungle.